VIOLINS
(PETER)

FLUTE
(THE BIRD)

OBOE
(THE DUCK)

BASSOON
(GRANDFATHER)

FRENCH HORN
(THE WOLF)

CLARINET
(THE CAT)

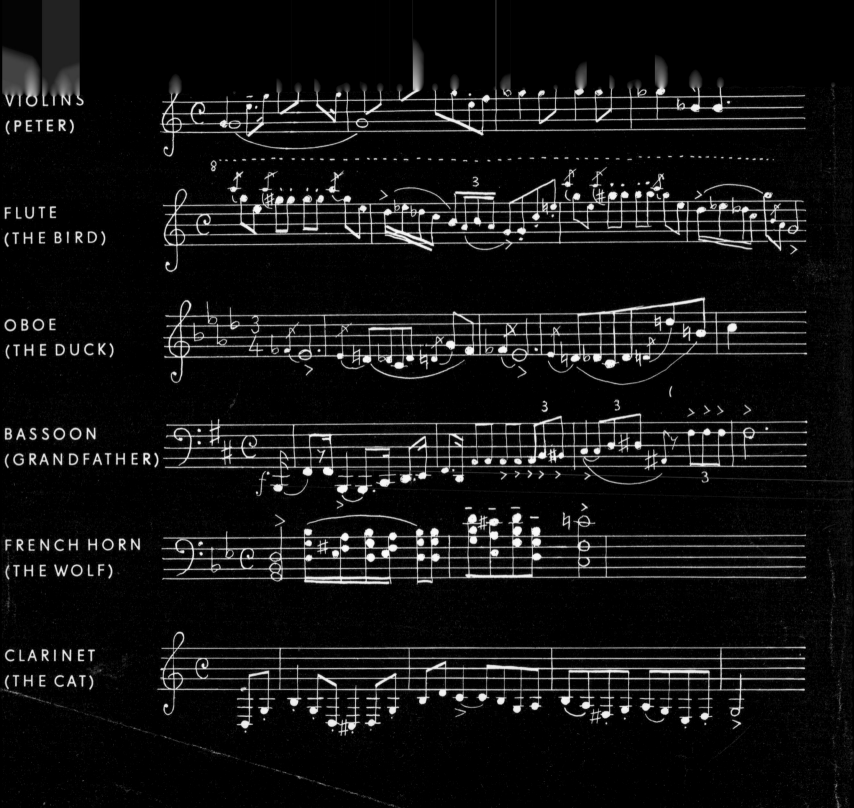

FRANKLIN WATTS INC · NEW YORK

Peter and the Wolf

SERGE PROKOFIEFF

ILLUSTRATED
BY FRANS HAACKEN

Library of Congress Catalog Card Number: 60–16759

German edition copyright 1958 by Alfred Holz Verlag, Berlin.

English text reproduced by kind permission of Messrs. Boosey & Hawkes, Ltd.

This English edition © 1961 by Bancroft & Co. (Publishers) Ltd. · All rights reserved

First published in Great Britain 1961 by Bancroft & Co. (Publishers) Ltd., Gordon House, Greencoat Place,
Westminster, London S. W. 1.

First American publication 1968 by Franklin Watts Inc., 575 Lexington Avenue, New York 22, New York, U.S.A.

Second American publication 1968 by Franklin Watts Inc., 575 Lexington Avenue, New York 22, New York, U.S.A.

Printed in Germany (U.S.S.R.)

It would be a shameful oversight to publish Serge Prokofieff's musical story of Peter outwitting the big gray wolf as a children's picture book, without also giving some mention of the music. This famous work, completed in 1936, is recognised as a little masterpiece. There is really no comparable piece of music which is so successful in leading children to good music, embodying as it does such a tremendous wealth of musical excellence.

With **Peter and the Wolf** Prokofieff created an entirely new musical art form. The more closely we listen to its highly original melodic content, the more we understand of the story and the clearer the tone-pictures become to us. They evoke the background of the story just as precisely as book illustrations do.

Every character is recognised by a definite motif, played on a characteristic musical instrument. Peter is gay and airy on the violin; contrasting with him is his slow and deliberate Grandfather on the bassoon; the flute plays the twittering bird; the oboe, the waddling duck; and the clarinet, the slinky, velvet-pawed cat. How can anyone fail to be impressed when, in the music, we hear the cat scrambling up the tree, or Peter letting down his rope? Serge Prokofieff had already begun to compose music at the age of five. When he died in March 1955, he was considered by music lovers throughout the world to be one of the finest of all Soviet artists. In **Peter and the Wolf,** as in his many children's piano pieces, he revealed his great tenderness towards children. The many recordings of this enchanting work testify to its tremendous popularity.

The Full Score, the **Hawkes Pocket Score,** a **Piano Solo Arrangement** and a **Complete Set of Parts** of the music are all obtainable from Boosey and Hawkes, Ltd., 295 Regent Street, London, W. I.

Early one morning
Peter opened the gate
and went out into
the big green meadow.

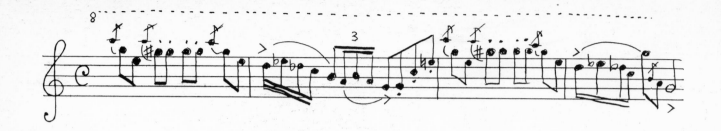

On a branch of
a big tree
sat a little bird,
Peter's friend.
"All is quiet,"
chirped the bird gaily.

Soon a duck
came waddling around.
She was glad that Peter
had not closed the
gate, and decided
to take a nice swim
in the deep pond
in the meadow.
Seeing the duck, the
little bird flew down
upon the grass,
settled next to her
and shrugged his
shoulders.

"What kind of bird
are you, if you can't
fly?" said he.
To this the duck
replied: "What kind of
bird are you, if
you can't swim?"
and dived
into the pond.
They argued and
argued, the duck
swimming in the
pond, the little bird
hopping along the shore.

Suddenly, something caught
Peter's eye:
he saw a cat crawling
through the grass.
The cat thought: "The bird
is busy arguing.
I'll just grab him."
Stealthily she crept
towards him
on her velvet paws.

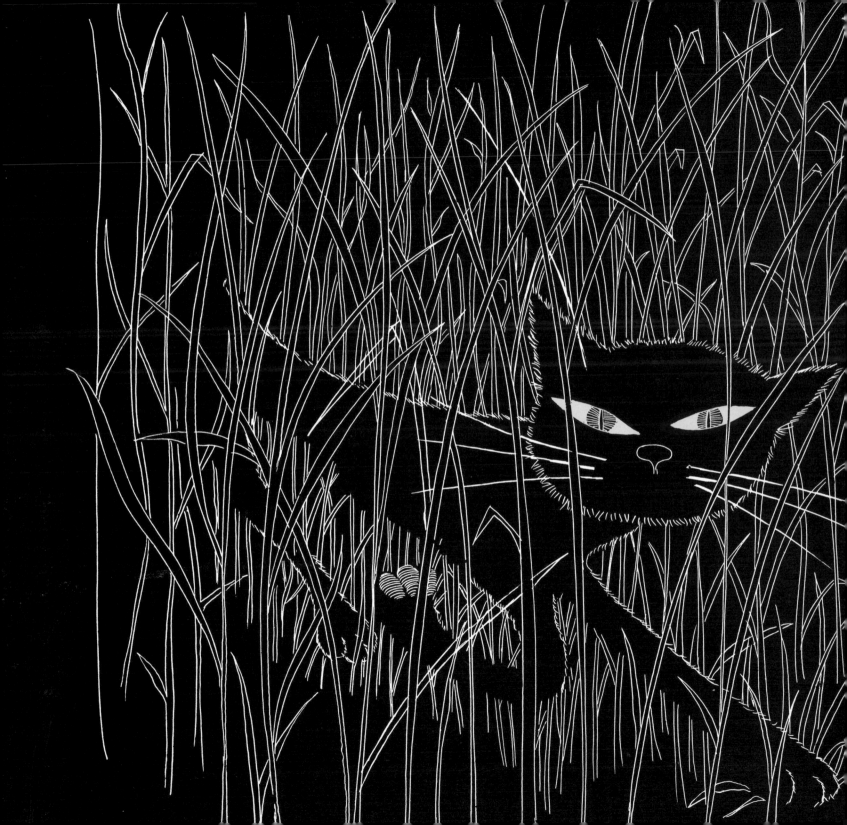

"Look out!" shouted
Peter, and the
bird immediately
flew up into the tree.

The duck quacked
angrily at the
cat from the
middle of the pond.

The cat crawled
around the tree
and thought:
"Is it worth
climbing up
so high? By the
time I get
there, the
bird will
have flown away."

Grandfather came out.
He was angry because
Peter had gone to the
meadow.
"It is a dangerous
place. If a wolf should
come out of the
forest, then what would
you do?"

Peter paid no
attention to his
Grandfather's words.
Boys such as he
are not afraid
of wolves.
But Grandfather
took Peter
by the hand,
led him home,
and locked the gate.

No sooner had
Peter gone, than a
big gray wolf
came out of the
forest.
In a twinkling
the cat climbed
up the tree.

The duck quacked
and in her excitement
jumped out of the pond.
But no matter
how hard the
duck tried to run,
she couldn't
escape the wolf.
He was getting
nearer – and nearer –
catching up with her . . .

and then he got her,
and with
one
gulp,
swallowed her.

So this is how things
stood: the cat
was sitting on
one branch, the bird on
another — not too
close to the cat —

and the wolf walked
round and round
the tree,
looking up at
them,
with wicked, greedy
eyes.

In the meantime,
Peter, without
the slightest fear,
stood behind the
closed gate
watching all
that was going on.

He ran home,
took a strong rope
and climbed up the
high stone wall.
One of the branches of
the tree around which
the wolf was walking,
stretched out
over the wall.
Grabbing hold of the branch,
Peter lightly climbed
over into the tree.

Peter said to the
bird: "Fly down and
circle around
the wolf's head, but
take care that he
doesn't catch you."

The bird almost
touched the wolf's head
with his wings,
while the wolf
snapped angrily
at him from
this side and that.
How that bird
did worry the wolf!
How he wanted to catch
him! But
the bird was cleverer,
and the wolf
simply
couldn't do anything
about it.

Meanwhile Peter
made a lasso,
and, letting
it
down,
caught the wolf
by the tail
and pulled with
all his might.
Feeling himself
caught, the wolf
began to jump wildly,
trying to get loose.
But Peter had tied the
other end of the rope
to the tree
and the wolf's
jumping only made
the rope around his tail
tighter.

Just then
the hunters
came out of the woods,
following the wolf's trail
and shooting as they went.

But Peter,
sitting in the tree,
said: "Don't shoot!
The bird and I have
already caught the wolf.
Now help us take
him to the
zoo."

Now just
imagine the
triumphant
procession:
Peter at the head,
followed by the hunters
leading the wolf.
And winding up the
procession
came Grandfather
and the
cat.

The procession is so long that we cannot get it all on one page

Grandfather
tossed his head
discontentedly:
"Well," he said,
"and if Peter
hadn't caught
the wolf, what
then?"

Above them flew
the bird,
chirping merrily:
"My, what fine ones we are,
Peter and I.
Look what we have
caught!"

And if one listened
carefully,
one could just hear
the duck
quacking inside the wolf,
because the wolf,
in his hurry,
had swallowed
her
whole.

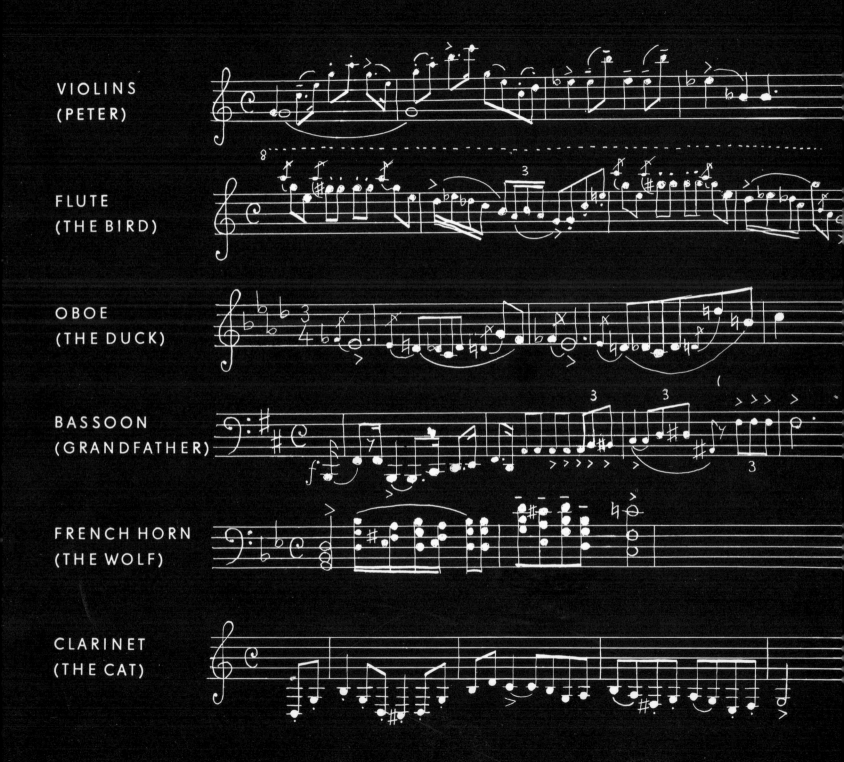